Hello Kitty is... Little Red Riding Hood

First published in the UK by HarperCollins *Children's Books* in 2014
1 3 5 7 9 10 8 6 4 2
ISBN: 978-0-00-753108-0

Written by Neil Dunnicliffe
Designed by Anna Lubecka

www.harpercollins.co.uk

Printed and bound in China

Hello Kitty is...

Little Red Riding Hood

HarperCollins *Children's Books*

The

Hello Kitty is...

Little Red Riding Hood

Dear Daniel is...

the naughty Mr Wolf

Mimmy is...

Mother

Jody is...

Father

Cast

Fifi is...

Granny

Thomas is...

Ben

Tippy and Tracy are...

the cake-eating friends!

Hello Kitty and her friends
are very excited. They are
performing in a new play.

The stage is set, the cast are ready and the audience are taking their seats.

Ladies and gentlemen, girls and boys, it's time for...

Little Red Riding Hood!

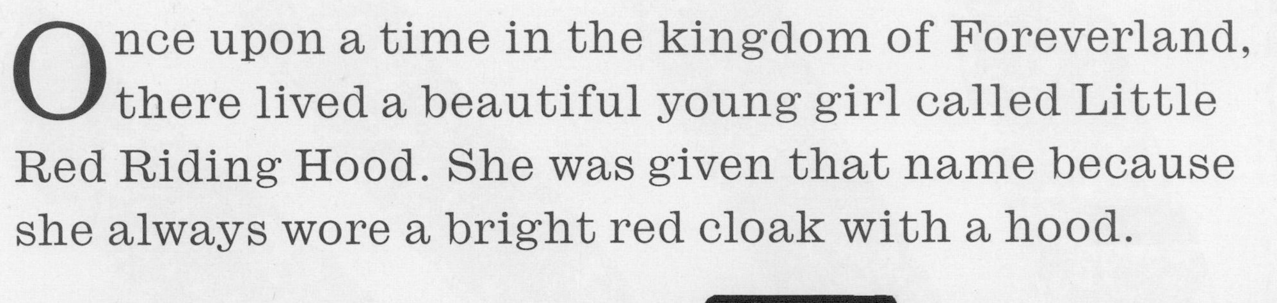

Once upon a time in the kingdom of Foreverland, there lived a beautiful young girl called Little Red Riding Hood. She was given that name because she always wore a bright red cloak with a hood.

The cottage that she shared with her mother, father and brother, Ben, was on the edge of a big, dark forest.

On the other side of the big,
dark forest lived Little Red
Riding Hood's granny, who
she loved very much.

One fine morning, Little Red Riding Hood set off for Granny's house. She was carrying a large basket of scrummy ingredients because they were going to spend the day baking.

"Don't forget to be careful and keep to the path," called her father, as Little Red Riding Hood entered the woods.

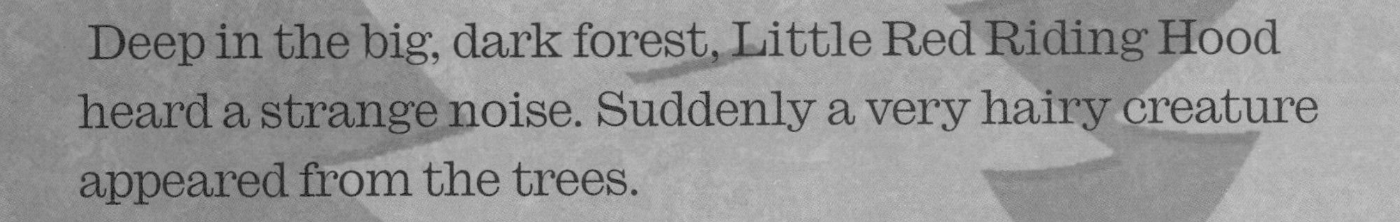

Deep in the big, dark forest, Little Red Riding Hood heard a strange noise. Suddenly a very hairy creature appeared from the trees.

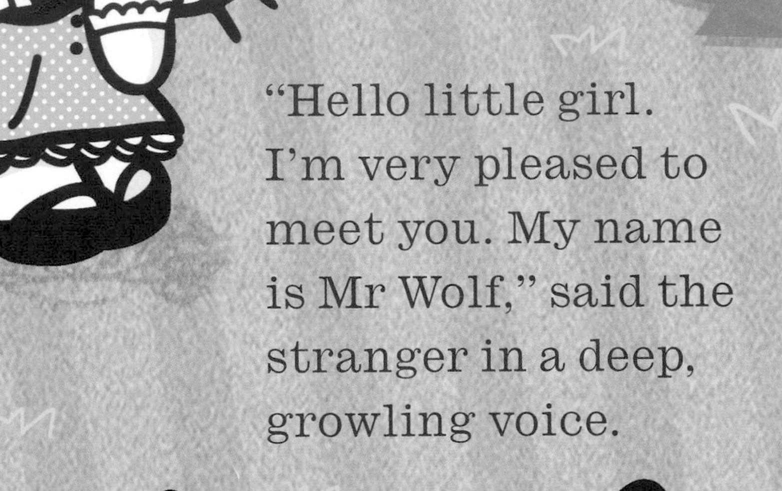

"Hello little girl. I'm very pleased to meet you. My name is Mr Wolf," said the stranger in a deep, growling voice.

Little Red Riding Hood looked scared.

"Don't be worried. I'm not the same as the other wolves," he explained. "I don't *usually* eat little girls, or grandmas. I much prefer eating cakes. Lots and lots of lovely freshly-baked cakes. Where are you going, little girl?"

Not wanting to tell a lie, Little Red Riding Hood said, "I'm walking to see my granny. We're going to, erm, spend some time together..."

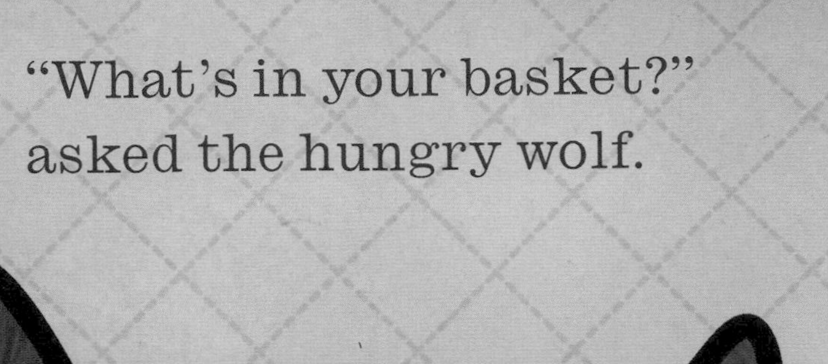

"What's in your basket?"
asked the hungry wolf.

"I'm taking Granny some
food for her larder," said
Little Red Riding Hood.

Sugar

The wolf sneaked a peek in the basket and spied all the scrummy ingredients. He suddenly felt very hungry for cake.

Growwwllll!

went Mr Wolf's tummy.

The wolf dashed back into the woods and ran to Granny's house.

He rang
the doorbell.

Ding Dong Ding Dong

When the door opened, the wolf
pushed his way into the cottage.

He shoved Granny into the larder and locked the door.

Grabbing a spare apron and glasses, he disguised himself as Granny and waited in the kitchen.

Little Red Riding Hood arrived at Granny's cottage. She rang the doorbell.

Ding Dong Ding Dong

The door creaked open. In the kitchen was Granny, although she didn't look *quite* like herself somehow.

Little Red Riding Hood felt a little suspicious.

"Let's start baking!" said Little Red Riding Hood. "First we'll make chocolate cake, then gingerbread, then lemon cake, then cornflake crispies, then..."

The wolf couldn't help himself; he growled loudly with delight.

Growwwlllll!

All those cakes, and all for him!

Flour
Butter

"I'll mix the ingredients if you melt the chocolate, Granny," said Little Red Riding Hood.

The wolf got into a terrible mess with the chocolate. It was obvious he had never baked before.

MILK

Little Red Riding Hood looked over at Granny. She was feeling even more suspicious that all wasn't right.

"Oh Granny, what big ears you have!"

"All the better to hear you with, my dear," came the reply.

"Oh Granny, what big eyes you have!"

"All the better to see you with, my dear."

"Oh Granny, what big hands you have!"

"All the better to hug you with, my dear."

"Oh Granny, what big teeth you have!"

"All the better to eat every one of your scrummy cakes with, my dear," roared the wolf.

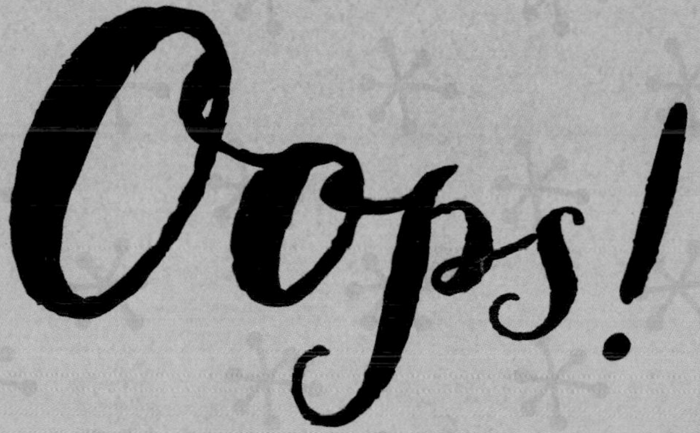
Oops!

Realising that the game was up, the wolf threw off the apron and glasses and started to chase Little Red Riding Hood around the kitchen.

Luckily, the wolf was just as hopeless at chasing as he was at baking.

He ran straight into the larder door and knocked it off its hinges. Out fell Granny.

Granny hit the wolf with her rolling pin.
He ran out of the door crying in pain.

Ouch!
Ooh!
Ow!

The wolf fled into the woods.

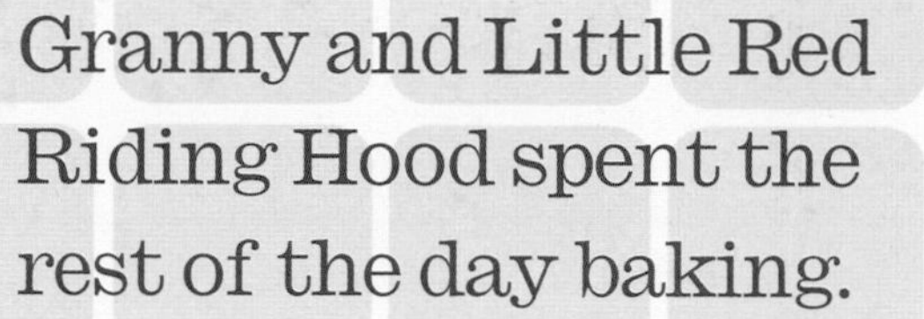

Granny and Little Red Riding Hood spent the rest of the day baking.

When Mother, Father and Ben arrived later, there were so many cakes they decided to have a tea party, and invited some friends, too.

While munching on her third slice of cake, Granny saw the wolf through the window. He said he was very sorry and promised never to be naughty again. Granny gave him a big slice of chocolate cake.

"I'll teach you how to bake too, as you've promised to be good," she said.

After many lessons with Granny, the wolf became an excellent baker. He opened a cake stall in the forest, which was very popular.

Everyone agreed that Mr Wolf's cakes were delicious, particularly his chocolate cake.

The End

Cheers and whoops sound out around the hall. The play is a wonderful success.

Hooray!
Hooray!

Hooray!

Hello Kitty bows as the applause rings out. "All that acting has made me peckish," she thinks. "It's time for a big piece of chocolate cake. And maybe some gingerbread too.

And perhaps some lemon cake after that. Mmmmm..."

The world of

Hello Kitty

Enjoy all of these wonderful Hello Kitty books.

Picture books

Hello Kitty is...
Little Red Riding Hood
A Hello Kitty fairy tale

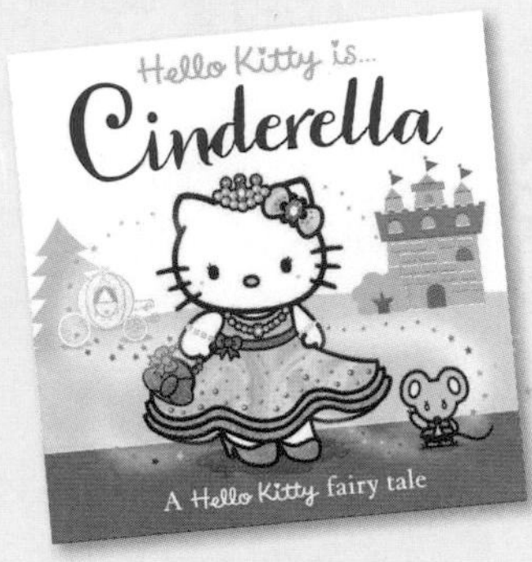
Hello Kitty is...
Cinderella
A Hello Kitty fairy tale

Activity books

HELLO KITTY
Wipe Clean Games
PINK INK!
With play and wipe pages!

HELLO KITTY
My Best Bumper Colouring Book
Colour, colour, colour with Hello Kitty!

HELLO KITTY
Dress Up Sticker Book:
Pretty in Pink
PINK
Dress Hello Kitty in pink, pink, pink!

HELLO KITTY
Dress Up Dolls
Plus over 100 press-out fashion items!

...and more!

Where's Hello Kitty?

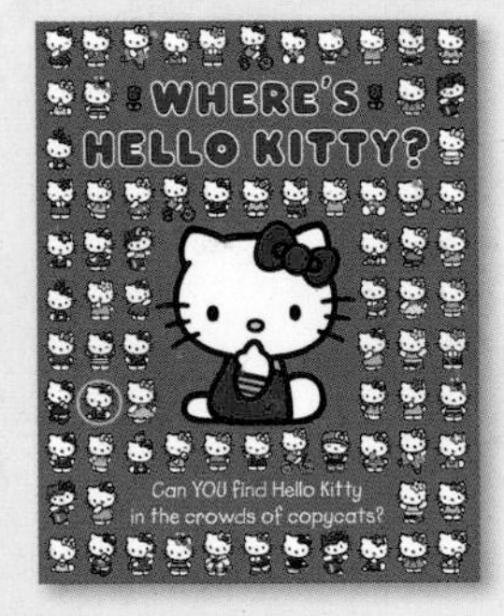
WHERE'S HELLO KITTY?
Can YOU find Hello Kitty in the crowds of copycats?

WHERE'S HELLO KITTY?
Fashion Star
Can YOU spot Hello Kitty amongst the fashion crowds?

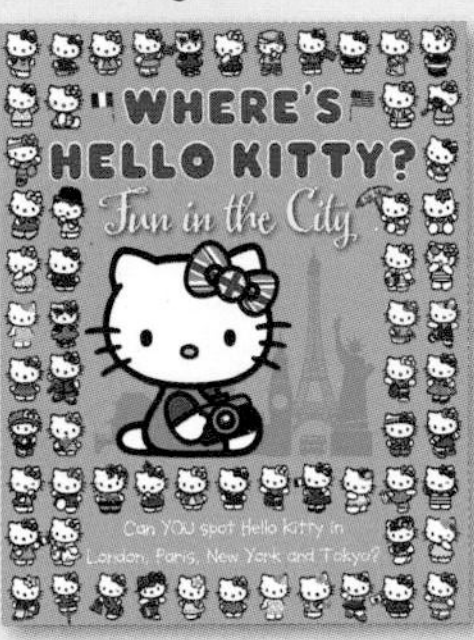
WHERE'S HELLO KITTY?
Fun in the City
Can YOU spot Hello Kitty in London, Paris, New York and Tokyo?

Hello Kitty and friends story book series

HELLO KITTY
and friends
The Friendship Club

HELLO KITTY
and friends
The School Trip

A HELLO KITTY STORY
HELLO KITTY
and friends
The Summer Fair

HELLO KITTY
and friends
The Pop Princess

A HELLO KITTY STORY
HELLO KITTY
and friends
The Wedding Day

HELLO KITTY
The Beach Holiday

HELLO KITTY
and friends
The Treasure Hunt

A HELLO KITTY STORY
HELLO KITTY
and friends
The Talent Show